Bamboo & Friends
The
Rainy Day

by Felicia Law
illustrated by Nicola Evans

Editor: Jacqueline A. Wolfe
Page Production: Tracy Davies
Creative Director: Keith Griffin
Editorial Director: Carol Jones
Managing Editor: Catherine Neitge

First American edition published in 2006 by
Picture Window Books
5115 Excelsior Boulevard
Suite 232
Minneapolis, MN 55416
877-845-8392
www.picturewindowbooks.com

Printed in the United States of America.

Library of Congress Cataloging-in-Publication Data
Law, Felicia.
The rainy day / by Felicia Law ; illustrated by Nicola
Evans.— 1st American ed.
p. cm. — (Bamboo & friends)
Summary: Three friends, sitting on a log in the magical forest,
consider what to do about the rain.
ISBN 1-4048-1280-6 (hardcover)
[1. Rain and rainfall—Fiction. 2. Rain forest animals—Fiction.]
I. Evans, Nicola, ill. II. Title. III. Series.
PZ7.L41835Ra 2005
[E]—dc22   2005007184

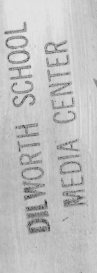

Bamboo, Velvet, and Beak sit on their log in the middle of the magical forest, just as they always do.

It rains every day in the magical forest. Rain falls every afternoon.

4

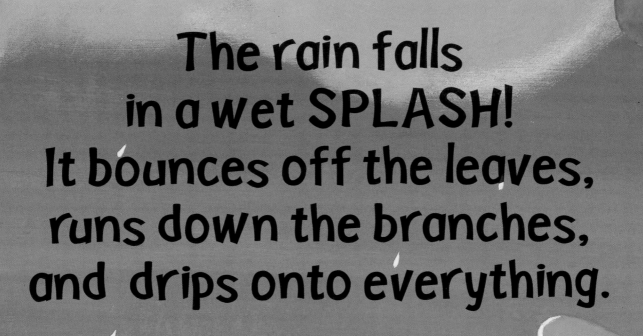

The rain falls
in a wet SPLASH!
It bounces off the leaves,
runs down the branches,
and drips onto everything.

In some tropical countries, the rainy season lasts seven months out of the year.

5

It pitter-patters
on the friends. It dribbles
down their necks.

It makes large puddles at their feet.

"Why?" asks Bamboo.

"Why what?"
asks Velvet.

9

"Why does it rain
every day?" asks Bamboo.

11

"It's that cloud," says Beak.

12

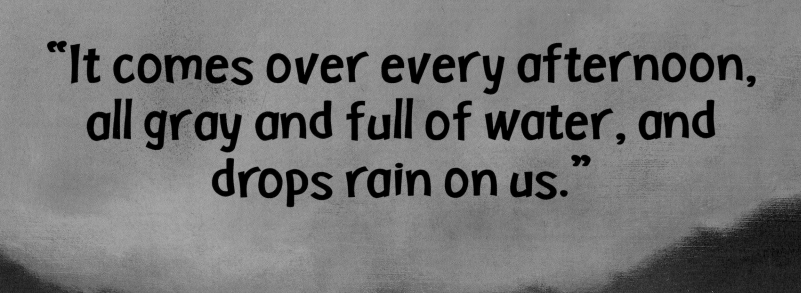

"It comes over every afternoon, all gray and full of water, and drops rain on us."

It rains when clouds are too heavy with moisture.

13

"And we always get wet," adds Beak, "because we always sit here, under the cloud."

A giant panda has thick, oily, wooly, waterproof fur that keeps it warm when it rains in the mountains.

"So why don't we sit somewhere else?" asks Velvet.

"We could sit over there where the colorful birds sit."

17

"They get wet, too,"
says Beak.
"They get soaked."

"Well, if we have to get wet," says Bamboo, "we might as well get wet sitting here!"

The more moisture there is in a cloud, the darker it appears.

21

"Together!"
adds Velvet.
"We might
as well all get
wet together."

Fun Facts

- In the tropical countries of India and Southeast Asia, there is heavy rainfall, especially during the summer. This rainy season is called the monsoon.

- Clouds are full of tiny drops of water.

- When clouds get too full to hold all of the water, the drops fall out of the clouds and it rains.

- Zebras take dust or mud baths to get clean instead of a bath with water!

- The zebras' habitat is the grassy plains, or savannas, of Africa.

- Waterproof feathers help keep puffins warm and dry.

- During winter, the bills and feet of puffins fade to a dull yellow. Every spring, their beaks and feet turn a colorful orange.

On the Web

FactHound offers a safe, fun way to find Internet sites related to this book. All of the sites on FactHound have been researched by our staff.

Here's how:

1. Visit www.facthound.com

2. Type in this special code for age-appropriate sites: 1404812806

3. Click on the FETCH IT button.

Your trusty FactHound will fetch the best sites for you!

Look for all of the books about Bamboo & Friends:

Marvelous Meals   The Flower's Busy Day
The Bookseller Bird   The Moon
The Creeping Vine   The Rainy Day
The Dragonfly   The Tree